ISBN-13: 978-1500956578
ISBN-10: 1500956570
Story by Barbara Miller
Book Illustrations by Inga Shalvashvili
Book Design by Adrian Navarrete

Lily Lemon Blossom

Twists, Twirls and Curls

Story by Barbara Miller
Illustrations by Inga Shalvashvili

Lily Lemon Blossom received a play hair styling kit from her Auntie Fran last week. So she and her friend Myra will be having a dolly hair day… And we get to take a peek.

They have two chairs in which their dolls will sit, and a little purple table with all their hair fixings on it. There are combs, brushes, dryers and clips, little rollers, big rollers for curls and flips. There are mirrors, headbands, ribbons and flowers. All that is needed to keep the girls busy for hours.

The dolls all sat in the pink polka dot chair waiting their turn... Daisy, Sweetpea, Willow and Fern.

Daisy and Fern's hair was shampooed by Myra. She then combed and brushed their hair and sat them under the dryer.

Sweetpea's hair was straightened with two side twirls. Willow's hair was full of rollers, she wanted lots of curls.

Lily's Big Baby Bear wanted long lashes to flutter for her beautiful dark eyes. And in her hair, tiny flowers full of colors piled high.

Addy the aardvark and Juddy
the giraffe quickly disappear,
when they see bunny rabbit
getting rollers on his ears.

They took time out
for a snack of fresh
fruits and berries,
slices of apples and
bright red cherries.
They ate, laughed and
talked about their
day, then gathered
the dolls together to
continue their play.

Myra added
a little more
color here and
there. Lily added a
few extra brushes to Daisy's
hair. Fern wanted just one
long curl with a ribbon of
green. It was ever so pretty,
she felt just like a queen.

The dolls looked oh so pretty and it was all so much fun. The girls were pleased with the work they had done.

"I have a great idea," said Myra, as she put the playthings back into their cases. "Why don't we do each other's hair and makeup each other's faces?"

"Sounds like fun," said Lily. "And when we're all done, we'll take pictures and show them to everyone."

Lily wanted her hair straightened with flips on the ends. Blue polish on her nails with tiny stars on them.

Myra wanted a bang
and two pony tails.
A little blush on her
cheeks, with pink and
blue polish on her nails.

Now it was time for picture taking.
Time to see the results of today's
merry making.

The girls and dolls sat in
the pink polka dot chair,
as the camera clicked and
took pictures of lovely
faces and hair.

Myra had an idea for
one more style that
was sure to make
everyone smile.

The two friends had a wonderful
time today. What a fun way for
little ones to play.

The End

Lily Lemon Blossom

Children's Picture Books
Collect Them All

Visit Lily at:

www.lilylemonblossom.com

Made in the USA
San Bernardino, CA
25 November 2015